THE DJINN IN THE SKULL

Stories from hidden Morocco

by

SAMANTHA HERRON

SOUL BAY PRESS
LONDON EASTBOURNE SYDNEY
MMXV

SOUL BAY PRESS LTD

Soul Bay Press Limited
3rd Floor Map House
34-36 St Leonards Road
Eastbourne
East Sussex
BN21 3UT

Registered in England No: 06322122
Registered office as above

First Edition 2015

Cover/Illustrations © Alan Stepney
Cover photograph © Alan Stepney
Typesetting by Alan Stepney

Soul Bay Press Logo © Alan Stepney & Andrew Franks

Printed and bound in United Kingdom by Anthony Rowe,
CPI Group (UK) Ltd, Croydon, CR0 4YY

A CIP catalogue for this book is available from the British Library

ISBN: 978-0-9574793-4-0

In memory of Aicha

رحمة الله عليها

ما كاين هروب من المكتوب

There is no escaping your destiny

CONTENTS

BACK FROM THE DEAD

Lahsen walked up the path leading to his neighbour's house, his skinny frame weighed down by the heavy goods on his back. The neighbour appeared at his front door and frowned when he saw his latest visitor. For Lahsen was well known for his relentless bartering and this neighbour had grown weary of the routine.

'Peace be upon you and the mercy of God and His blessing!' proclaimed Lahsen.

'And upon you,' the neighbour responded politely.

'How are you my brother? Still blessed with your health, God willing?'

'I'm well, thanks be to God,' the neighbour replied.

'And your mother and father?' Lahsen pressed on.

'They're well, thanks be to God.'

'And your cousin, is he recovered now?'

The neighbour took a breath. 'He is well, thanks

be to God.'

'Ah yes,' said Lahsen, 'we do indeed thank God when we have our health. May God be with us during these difficult times.'

'Just what is it that you want today Lahsen?' the neighbour interrupted, eager to get this over with and see Lahsen on his way.

'I've come to do a little exchange with you,' said Lahsen. 'I will hand over the treasures that I've brought with me and you can give me your donkey in return.'

The neighbour sighed. He had no intention of exchanging goods with Lahsen today or any other day, and he certainly was not going to part with his hard-working donkey.

He looked Lahsen in the eye. 'I'm afraid I can't help you today,' he said, 'for my donkey is dead.'

Lahsen returned the neighbour's stare, as there came from behind the house the unmistakable sound of a donkey braying. Lahsen cried out, 'There is no God but God and Mohamed is His prophet. Oh my brother,' he pleaded, 'if your donkey is dead, then please, God preserve us, tell me who or what is making that sound?'

'Why my dear brother,' the neighbour smiled, 'can it be that you never learned that animals continue to call out to us long after they have died? My poor donkey is buried right here in front of the house, but not a day goes by when I don't hear him call out to me.'

Lahsen looked down at the spot where the donkey was buried. He had indeed never before heard of such a thing and he wasn't sure that he was entirely comfortable with the idea. But if this was God's will, then he must give praise and ask forgiveness.

'Forgive me Lord and forgive me brother,' he said, 'I am so sorry to have troubled you. May God protect and preserve you.'

A bemused Lahsen reloaded his baggage onto his back and shuffled his way down the neighbour's pathway.

A few weeks later this same neighbour had to leave town to visit his family in the mountains. He untied his donkey so that it would be free to roam and graze in the fields surrounding the house, and he set off as the call for the dawn prayer sounded. Later that same morning Lahsen was walking past the neighbour's house, on his way to barter some new goods in the Jewish kasbah, when he heard the neighbour's donkey deliver a proud and bellowing bray.

Lahsen's eyes glazed over and his legs began to quiver. 'There is no God but God and Mohamed is His prophet,' he whispered. He turned to face the house and his hand flew to his mouth when he saw the donkey.

'God is the greatest, God is the greatest!' he cried

and dropped to his knees in prostration. 'My Lord I seek refuge with you, lest the Devil should come near me.'

Lahsen breathed deeply. Then he slowly got to his feet and walked over to where the donkey was standing. Taking great care not to look into the donkey's eyes, he reached out and took hold of the rope around its neck. Pulling very gently he lead the donkey to the front door of the house and secured the rope. He then walked round the back of the house, to the den where he knew his neighbour kept his tools. He picked out a large shovel and came back round to the front.

Lahsen looked up at the sky. 'In the name of God, the most gracious, the most merciful,' he said and set to work digging.

He worked without pausing, oblivious to the heat of the sun. When he had finished he put the shovel to one side and walked over to the donkey. Again mindful to avert his eyes, he untied the rope and gently walked the donkey over to where he had been digging.

'In the name of God, the most gracious, the most merciful,' he repeated and jumped down into the grave. He carefully coaxed the donkey down beside him and eased it into a sleeping position. When he was satisfied that the donkey was asleep, he climbed back out and quickly covered the donkey with the earth that he had removed.

A few days later Lahsen was again walking past the neighbour's house, on his way to barter goods in a nearby village. He stopped when he heard his neighbour cry out to him.

'Why Lahsen! Peace be upon you my brother!'

'And upon you peace,' replied Lahsen.

'Have you got a minute?' the neighbour asked.

Lahsen put down his load and walked up the path. 'I always have a minute to spare for a brother or sister. How can I be of service?'

'I have just returned from a trip to the mountains,' the neighbour began.

'We thank God for your safe return,' Lahsen interrupted.

'We thank God, yes,' the neighbour went on, 'but a very strange thing has happened. My donkey hasn't called out to me since I returned.'

Lahsen smiled and nodded. 'You have nothing to fear my brother,' he said, 'I will put your mind at rest, God willing. A few days ago, when you were away on your travels, I was walking past your house and I heard your poor donkey crying out. It was just as you had described. Only when I looked up, I saw that he had somehow escaped from his grave. I swear to God I saw him just as clearly as I see you now, roaming in the field in front of your house. I don't mind saying that I was a little unnerved. But by the grace of God I knew what I had to do. So I took the liberty of searching out your shovel and dug another grave for him just here. May God and your good self forgive me both. But your donkey is at rest now brother. I do not think you will be hearing from him again.'

Lahsen shook his neighbour's hand and patted him on the shoulder. He made his way down the path, hoisted his sack onto his back and disappeared from view.

The neighbour slowly turned his head and stared down at the earth where his donkey now lay buried.

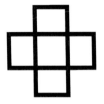

MISSING

Ali was resting in the shade of an acacia tree on the edge of the desert, watching the man who was limping towards him. When he was near enough to make eye contact, he invited the man to sit beside him. The man sat down in front of Ali, hunching his shoulders and holding his head at a strange angle.

'Peace be upon you,' said Ali.

'And upon you peace,' the man replied.

'My name's Ali.'

'Mohamed.'

Mohamed's hands and face were dirty and deeply tanned. He was unnaturally thin and much younger than Ali had at first thought. Underneath his beard and long knotted hair, Ali could see the face of a young man.

Mohamed was staring at the ground. He seemed dazed and reluctant to look at Ali.

'Have you come from the sands?' Ali asked him. Mohamed nodded.

'Your family lives in the sands?'

'No,' said Mohamed, 'I don't live with my family. I'm wandering alone through the sands.'

Mohamed had nothing with him, not even a carrier bag. His thin cotton shirt and trousers were badly torn, even for a nomad.

Ali tried to catch his eye. 'What do you do for food and water Mohamed?'

Mohamed shrugged. 'I eat and drink whatever camels eat and drink.'

Ali pulled out of his rucksack a chunk of bread filled with goat meat and handed it to Mohamed. He nodded his thanks and ate a little of it, but it seemed an effort for him to chew and swallow. Ali handed him a bottle of water and then pulled out another chunk of bread and goat meat for himself. He took a large bite and spoke with a full mouth, 'So where does your family live?'

Mohamed drank from the bottle and then looked around as though he was searching for something. 'They live in the north. Look, I need to be on my way.'

'On your way to where?' asked Ali.

'To the border.'

Ali stopped eating and looked at Mohamed. The sands by the border were known to conceal mines and smugglers crossing over from the east. If Ali let

Mohamed go there, he could be sending him to his death.

He looked at Mohamed. 'I'm taking you home with me first,' he said. 'You need to eat and sleep before you head off again.'

Mohamed didn't say anything as he slowly got to his feet.

Ali's wife Fatima openly cried when she saw Mohamed walk through the door. Not since her days growing up in the desert had she seen someone so close to dying from a simple lack of food. She and Ali lead him into the lounge, where she arranged some cushions and blankets for him in the corner of the room. Mohamed lay down, but he didn't close his eyes.

'Would you like to watch the news Mohamed?' Fatima switched on the television and flicked through several channels until she found the lunchtime bulletin. She stood and listened to the headlines and then left the room.

She returned carrying a tray with a bowl of stew and bread and water on it. She placed it in front of Mohamed and sat down next to him. Mohamed ate some small pieces of the bread, which he dipped in the juices of the stew. But when Fatima offered him a chunk of bread which she had filled with lamb, he shook his head.

'I no longer feel like eating meat,' he said.

Fatima didn't say anything. She got up and placed a small table in front of Ali, then quietly left the room.

'Mohamed,' said Ali, 'you are not a camel, you are a man and a man needs to eat meat if he is going to spend his days walking in the sands.'

Fatima came back into the room carrying another tray. She placed it on the table in front of Ali and turned to Mohamed.

'If you've had enough to eat Mohamed,' she said, 'there's a kettle full of hot water in the bathroom. I've also left a change of clothes for you. Come with me.'

Mohamed stood and followed her out of the room.

Ali ate his lunch as he stared at the adverts on the television. He wondered what sequence of events had brought Mohamed to where he was today, whether he was missed by anyone. Ali had often thought of running away from home when he was a young boy. He had watched his parents struggle to feed him and his younger brothers and sisters and had felt that he was wasting his time going to school. For a while he had considered heading to the nearest big town to try to find work.

Mohamed came back into the room and sat down on the cushions that Fatima had arranged for him. His hair was wet, but he was still wearing his own clothes.

Fatima followed him in. 'Mohamed,' she said,

'it's only a few days till Eid, why don't you stay and spend it with us?'

Mohamed looked towards her. 'I think it's time to go home.'

'For that we thank God,' said Fatima. 'But you'd be honouring us if you would stay and celebrate Eid with us first.'

Mohamed stood and he shook his head at Fatima. 'I must go home,' he said. He turned towards Ali. 'Could you give me the money to buy a ticket for the coach? I don't have anything.'

'Yes of course,' said Ali. 'If you're certain that's what you want?'

Mohamed nodded.

'Do you mean today? Now?'

Mohamed nodded.

Ali and Mohamed took a taxi to the coach station. They were both silent as they drove through the quiet streets of the town. When they arrived at the station Mohamed insisted that Ali stay in the taxi. He took enough money to buy himself a ticket, but would take no more.

'Thank you,' said Mohamed. 'I thank you and your wife.'

'I wish you a safe journey,' said Ali, 'and a happy reunion with your family, God willing.'

When Mohamed didn't say anything else, Ali reluctantly turned his head and asked the taxi driver to take him home.

In the weeks that followed Ali and Fatima would often remember Mohamed and wonder aloud what had happened to him. Then one evening they were eating dinner in front of the television, watching the latest appeal from the popular series *Missing*. A young girl appeared on the screen, sitting between an elderly woman and a middle-aged man. She spoke into the camera:

'We're looking for my brother Mohamed,' she said, 'who is twenty years old and walks with a limp. He disappeared from our home eighteen months ago and we don't know why. There was no argument or falling out and he's never been in any kind of trouble.'

The camera cut to the elderly woman, who was crying. 'He's always been my favourite son,' she said in a quiet voice. 'Mohamed was never like the other boys, getting into trouble with drugs or stealing or girls. I don't know why he ran away. Why would he do this to me?'

Mohamed's mother broke down and the man sitting on the other side of her daughter came into shot. 'I'm Mohamed's eldest brother,' he said and then paused. 'I need you to understand that Mohamed is young in his mind. There are many things in the adult world which he doesn't understand. We're worried that he might be in danger if he's living on the streets. Please, if you know where he is,' he paused again. 'Please get in touch with us.' He turned away from the camera and looked towards his mother. 'I don't think our poor mother can bear this for much longer.'

The camera pulled back to show Mohamed's mother, brother and sister sitting together and then cut to a studio portrait of Mohamed, dressed smartly in a black and white striped djellaba.

Fatima let out a strange sound and stared at the screen, as tears ran down her face.

LARBI BRINGS THE NEWS

Khadija poured out two glasses of tea, one for Izza and one for herself. She drank hers down noisily, as Izza listened to the footsteps approaching the house. A man appeared at the doorway and walked into the middle of the room. He looked like a child who happened to find himself inside an old man's body.

'Ikh! Larbi! Take off your sandals!' Khadija scolded him. 'Put them outside, then you can come and sit with me and have a glass of tea.'

Khadija shook her head at Izza, as Larbi left the room and then rushed back in with dirty bare feet.

'Savaban savaban?'

He first shook hands with Khadija and then Izza, repeating 'Savaban savaban?'

'Savaban?' asked Izza.

'Apparently he's greeting us in French,' Khadija explained.

'There's been an accident!' Larbi shouted excitedly. 'In front of the market near the baker's, between a taxi and a small van. Rashid says the taxi driver might die.'

Khadija frowned at Izza. 'What accident Larbi? Don't be silly, there's been no accident.'

'There has!' he insisted. 'They took the taxi driver away in an ambulance. Rashid says he lives on the farm behind his uncle.'

'Maybe there has been an accident?' offered Izza.

Khadija sighed. 'I'm surprised there's anyone left in this town,' she said, 'the way Larbi goes around announcing the deaths of everyone. Only God knows whether what he says is true.'

'Here!' Larbi thrust a paper note at Khadija. 'How much is this worth?'

'Where on earth did you get this from?' asked Khadija, looking at Izza. 'It's a hundred dirham note.'

'A hundred?' Larbi thought for a moment. 'Is that enough to buy a cassette player from the market?'

'Who gave you this money?' asked Khadija, ignoring his question.

'An American wearing a blue hat. He had a little beard,' he said, stroking the middle of his chin.

'You shouldn't be talking to Americans,' warned Khadija, 'or they'll take you away and lock you up and we might never see you again.'

'I'm not crazy,' said Larbi.

'Of course not,' said Khadija, winking at Izza.

'They inject you with poison if they think you're crazy,' he explained to Izza. 'Savaban savaban?' He picked up Khadija's phone and held it to his ear. 'Allo allo? Adil called last night. He got married and left home, so it's my turn next.'

'Have you found yourself a pretty girl?' asked Izza kindly.

'Maybe,' he said.

'His mother died when he was three years old,' said Khadija, 'and his father remarried a devil of a woman. She's never been able to love poor Larbi. Now his father has passed away, God rest his soul, and his brothers have all left home and it's just Larbi and the step-mother. God only knows what his future will be.'

'I'm going to get married,' said Larbi. 'It's my turn to get married.'

'God willing,' said Khadija. 'But weddings are expensive and you'll have to look after your wife when you're married.'

'I don't think we'll need much money,' he said smiling.

'Are you going to stay and have lunch with us today Larbi?' asked Izza.

Larbi shook his head.

'He won't stay unless it's Friday couscous,' explained Khadija. 'It's the only meal he can manage since he lost most of his teeth.'

Larbi looked intently at Khadija. 'Auntie Khadija,

don't look so sad. Why are you sad? You shouldn't worry about things. Life is hard.'

No one said anything.

'And death is hard,' he continued. 'Death is very hard. When my dad died I was patient and didn't cry.'

'God bless you,' said Khadija.

Larbi stood up and walked out of the room.

'He's gone to have a cigarette,' said Khadija. 'Poor soul, he's been this way since he was a child. Some say he was snatched from his mother's arms after he was born and replaced with a baby djinn. Others say he was a normal little boy, until he was bitten by a snake and his father couldn't get him to the hospital in time. Only God knows the truth.'

'Amen,' said Izza.

'Now he wants to get married so he can be a father. He says he wants to come home in the evening and hear his children calling out for Daddy.'

'Auntie Khadija?' Larbi stood at the doorway, holding his burning cigarette between his finger and thumb. He moved towards Izza. 'Savaban savaban?'

'Ikh! Take that dirty cigarette outside!' shouted Khadija.

Larbi giggled, but did as he was told. When he came back into the room he went and sat next to Izza.

'Esma's gone,' he told her.

'Who's Esma?' asked Izza.

'A blind woman who used to sit in front of the

hospital,' explained Khadija.

'Last night,' said Larbi. 'They took her away in a van in the middle of the night and drove her into the mountains.'

'God be with her,' said Khadija.

'They won't get me though, I won't let them. They only come for you when it's dark, so I'm going to move into the small room upstairs. Then if they come to the house at night, they won't know that I'm there.'

'God preserve you,' said Izza.

'I'm going to go to the market and buy a silver cassette player. Then tonight I'll move all my things into my new room and listen to music until I fall asleep. I won't leave my room again until the sun rises.'

Larbi moved closer to Izza. 'Savaban savaban? Come and have dinner with us tonight.'

'I'm sorry Larbi,' said Izza, 'I have to cook dinner for my own family tonight. But another time, God willing, I'd like that very much.'

He took a packet of cigarettes from his pocket and pulled one out.

'Goodbye then,' he said to Izza. 'Goodbye Auntie.'

'God help you,' said Izza.

'God help you,' said Khadija.

Larbi stood and walked out of the room. Khadija pulled the tray of tea glasses towards her and filled each dirty glass with warm water from the kettle. She handed Izza a small cloth and after she washed each glass, Izza dried and polished them.

'There's a little girl at the door,' whispered Izza.

Khadija looked up. 'Meryam?' she said, 'Are you on your own? Where's your mum?'

Meryam ran towards Khadija, then stopped in the middle of the room when she noticed Izza.

'Daddy's had an accident and Mummy won't stop crying,' she said.

Khadija held out her arms and Meryam ran into them. As she held the girl in a firm embrace, Khadija turned towards Izza and whispered, 'Her father drives a taxi in the town.'

THE DJINN IN THE SKULL

Hamid and his friends were playing in the dry riverbed at the edge of the village. Summer had arrived and a hot wind was blowing in from the east. Hamid kicked at the stones that lined the bottom of the riverbed, whilst he nibbled at the dried beans his mother had given to him when he left the house. His foot dislodged a large black stone and he let out a loud cry. 'By God,' he shouted to his friends, 'we're not alone!'

The boys huddled around their friend and found themselves staring into the empty eye sockets of a human skull. Hamid had been scared at first, his find catching him off guard. But now he laughed. 'Look, he's still got his teeth! I wonder if he's hungry?' His friends laughed too, as he took one of his mother's beans and tried to push it through the clenched teeth of the skull.

The boys quickly tired of their games and when the sun began to set they each made their way home. Hamid didn't have far to go and was soon walking through his front door. He greeted his mother and kissed his baby sister, then settled himself in front of the television to watch his favourite cartoon channel.

By the time his father returned home from work, Hamid was struggling to stay awake. He excused himself from dinner and wished his parents a good night. He had no energy to play with his friends or to watch television, so he climbed up onto the roof and made his bed. He quickly fell asleep.

In the early hours of the morning, when everyone in the village was sleeping soundly, Hamid woke suddenly in fear. He could see his parents and baby sister sleeping peacefully in front of him, bathed in the moon's white light. He listened for a moment to the familiar comforting sounds of his father snoring and the dogs barking in the distance. Twisting round to look out from the village across the sands, he froze when he saw an old man staring back at him.

'Shame on you boy,' the old man said calmly. 'May God forgive you.'

The man was wrapped in the thin white sheet of a pilgrim. It glowed brightly in the moonlight and Hamid found it hard to look directly at him.

'Who are you?' he asked, bringing his hand up to his forehead to shade his eyes from the glare.

'Who I am is not important,' the old man replied.

'I am simply a man.'

He pointed at Hamid with his index finger, then brought it to his lips as though warning him not to speak. 'Do you see my lips, boy? Do you know how many times the words of the Holy Quran have passed through these very lips? The words which God the Almighty sent down to our prophet Mohamed, may God's blessings be upon him. The words which I memorised in my boyhood and recited daily over the sick, the dying and the desperate.' He raised his voice, 'Do you know how many times?'

Hamid shook his head, too frightened to speak.

The man gestured over to where Hamid's parents and baby sister lay. 'May God protect you and your humble family from the whisperings of the Devil,' he said. Hamid looked over and saw that his mother, father and sister were still sleeping, apparently undisturbed by the old man's appearance. He turned back to speak to the old man. But he was gone.

The next morning Hamid woke earlier than usual and ate breakfast with his father. When his father left for work, Hamid went into the kitchen where his mother was kneading dough.

'Do we have a spare white sheet?' he asked her.

'There are some piled up on top of the blankets,' she replied, 'Why do you ask?'

37

'It's for a project at school,' said Hamid, 'I have to leave early today.'

Hamid ran up the steps onto the roof and picked out the cleanest white sheet he could find. Then he filled a small plastic bottle with water and put the bottle and the sheet into his satchel. Calling out to his mother that he was leaving, he retraced the path back down to the dry riverbed.

The skull was still there. It looked older and dirtier than he remembered.

He opened his satchel and took out the sheet and the bottle of water. He unfolded the sheet and spread it out on the ground. Then he carefully rinsed the skull with the water from the bottle, rubbing away the dust and clay which had gathered over time. He placed the cleaned skull in the middle of the sheet and wound the sheet around it.

Holding the wrapped skull close against his chest, he walked down into the valley of the riverbed. The large black stone, which until the day before had been sheltering the skull, was still lying where he and his friends had left it. Next to it he could see markings, showing where the skull must have laid in rest until he disturbed it.

Hamid lay the wrapped skull back in its place and gently eased the stone into its position. 'In God's name,' he said quietly. Then he walked back up the slope, picked up his satchel and carried on his way to school.

AZIZ GETS ENGAGED

Every year Aziz would travel down from the seaside town where he worked as a carpenter and spend Eid with his mother and brothers in the south. This year he announced before leaving that he was ready to get married and would like, God willing, to get engaged during the festive period. He asked his mother if she could find him a suitable girl. 'Her looks are not important,' he explained, 'but she must be a hard worker and ready to become part of our family.'

Aziz's mother was immediately on the phone to her sister, who still lived in the desert village where they had grown up. 'Find me a girl, a good girl from a God-fearing family,' she said, 'and we will come down after Eid to make her acquaintance.'

And so it was that three days after Eid, Aziz, his mother and four brothers arrived in the desert village. A girl had been found and her father had given his consent. It was now time for Aziz and the girl to meet and decide if they wished to become husband and wife.

The girl's family lived on the edge of a large palmerie some distance from the main road. Aziz, his mother, his aunt and four brothers all made their way along the narrow sandy paths that led up to the house. They found the girl's youngest sister waiting at the door to greet them. She welcomed everyone inside, ushering them towards the main room where the girl and her mother were preparing tea.

Aziz and his family filed in one by one, greeting first the mother and then the girl, before sitting on the opposite side of the room. The women eased into their familiar chat, enquiring after mutual friends and checking on the health of elderly relatives. The girl was joined by her youngest sister and together they circled the room, handing out glasses of strong sweet tea and Eid pastries.

Aziz watched his prospective bride tending to her guests. She made sure that everyone was supplied with something to eat and drink, before she seated herself between her mother and sister. Aziz let his eyes rest on her. She didn't flinch as she returned his gaze.

He turned away, sensing movement from his brothers beside him. They were laughing and nudging one another. The eldest winked at him. 'Do you like what you see, little brother?' he mouthed.

Aziz smiled and turned back to look at the girl. His mother had told him that choosing a wife is like buying fruit at the market. When you take the fruit home you will find out what lies beneath the skin. 'But whatever you find,' she advised, 'whether it pleases you or not, she is the wife that God chose for you.'

Aziz drained his glass and stood. He walked over to where the girl was sitting with her mother and sister and returned his glass to the silver tray. Aziz's mother was laughing and chatting with his aunt, but her eyes were on her son. He raised his left eyebrow at her and smiled. She returned his smile as she slowly got to her feet and, with a faint nod to her sister, left the room.

On the other side of the room the girl's mother had closely watched the exchange. Nodding to both her daughters, she too stood and left the room. Aziz and his brothers looked from one to the other and the room became quiet.

Then a loud throaty wail sounded outside the door and the two mothers walked back into the room smiling. Aziz's aunt jumped up, clapping her hands and filling the room with her high-pitched wailing. His mother walked over to her future daughter-in-law and proudly placed on her wedding finger the ring which Aziz had bought several weeks ago, in hope and trust. Then the girl's mother walked over to Aziz and sealed the contract by placing a ring on his wedding finger.

Aziz's mother and aunt trilled in jubilation, while his brothers hugged him one by one. The chatter between the women grew louder as everyone relaxed. Each of the brothers pulled out his mobile phone and took turns photographing his future sister-in-law, who was sitting quietly between her mother and sister on the other side of the room.

'We don't want Aziz forgetting what she looks like between now and the wedding,' the eldest brother laughed.

Aziz smiled and looked across at his future wife. She turned towards him and looked directly into his eyes. Only God knew what lay ahead for them. But Aziz knew that whatever happened, nothing would ever be the same.

THE DJINN IN THE TREE

Mouna and Sofia were sitting in Mouna's courtyard, removing the chaff from a large sack of wheat. The two women worked slowly and without pressure, rhythmically bouncing the grain in their baskets as they laughed and chatted.

In the distance there was the sound of a group of women wailing in grief. Mouna and Sofia both heard it, but didn't pay it much attention. They continued working and chatting, while the sound of the weeping grew louder as it approached the house. When the chorus of grief reached Mouna's front door, the two women put down their baskets and stared.

Mouna stood and went to open the door. She was pushed aside by five hysterical women, who rushed past her into the courtyard and fell to the ground weeping. Mouna felt a sharp pain in her left breast. Her body crumpled and she fell to the ground in front of the open door. As Sofia ran to her friend to take care of her, she noticed a boy standing perfectly framed in the doorway.

It transpired that the boy had been playing in a field by the canal when he had come across Mouna's son Mustafa sleeping at the foot of a palm tree. He said that a djinn had appeared at the top of the tree amongst the dates and leaves. The djinn, which the boy described as looking like a shrunken man, had skipped down the trunk of the tree and jumped onto the ground. It had hopped around Mustafa's legs and peered at his closed eyes and the boy had thought that Mustafa must surely be about to wake. Then the djinn had slapped Mustafa three times about the face and disappeared back up the tree.

The boy had watched Mustafa for a long time. When he didn't move or wake, the boy had gone to get help from his uncle who lived nearby. He told his uncle what had happened and the uncle asked the boy to stay in the house, while he went to the field to investigate. He found Mustafa lying at the foot of the palm tree, just as the boy had described. When he tried to rouse him he discovered that Mustafa was dead.

When the uncle returned home he found the house empty. The boy had set off for the village where Mustafa's family lived. By the time he arrived there, word of Mustafa's death had reached the women who lived on the edge of the village. He followed the sound of their weeping and walked into the house where they had congregated. The women immediately sensed who he was and gathered around him. They asked him to tell again what had happened and besieged him with questions.

But the boy refused to speak. He silently followed the women when they went to tell Mouna the terrible news and later he silently walked behind the men who lay Mustafa to rest.

But he never spoke again after telling his uncle what he had witnessed.

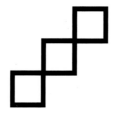

THE BLIND MAN

Hussein was blind, having lost his eyesight as a child. He had just finished praying the last prayer of the day and was sitting on his prayer mat thinking. He'd spent a quiet day at home while his wife Mama visited her friend Touria, who had been widowed a few years earlier and lived nearby.

Hussein was thinking that it was unusual for his wife not to have returned home by this hour. Her health wasn't good during these hot summer months and he was growing concerned. Mama and her friend both carried mobile phones, but for reasons known only to themselves they never bothered to switch them on. So Hussein would have to pay Touria a visit to see if his wife was still with her.

He got to his feet and rolled up his prayer mat. Then he picked up his stick and headed off up the mountain path. When he reached Touria's front door he couldn't hear any voices talking inside. So he walked around the house to the covered terrace at the back, where he knew Touria slept during the summer.

As he did so he wondered how he might find his wife without waking Touria or any other women who may be sleeping on the terrace. Mama was a big-boned woman, with a generous bust and large thighs. Hussein had of course never seen her likeness, but he knew every inch of her body by touch and loved her sweet smell.

An idea came to him. He lay his stick on the ground and got down onto his hands and knees. Then he slowly crawled along the edge of the terrace sniffing the air. He stopped when his knees nudged the body of a sleeping woman. He paused for a moment and then placed one hand on top of the woman's body. When she didn't stir, he carefully moved it around until it found her buttocks.

Feeling an absence of his wife's familiar fleshiness, he quickly removed his hand. He waited patiently and listened to the woman's breathing, until he was satisfied that she hadn't felt his interference. Then he continued crawling along the edge of the terrace sniffing the air.

When he brushed against a second sleeping woman, he felt more confident in his method and his hand quickly found the woman's thighs. They were reassuringly ample, but were more solid to the touch than those of his wife. And Hussein still couldn't detect his wife's sweet aroma. So he withdrew his hand and moved on once more.

As he rounded the corner of the terrace he came across the body of a third sleeping woman, who was hanging over the edge of the terrace blocking his passage. This time Hussein was careless and his hand promptly landed on top of the woman's breasts. He instantly knew that they didn't belong to his wife, for they were much smaller than hers. But he forgot himself for a moment and let his hand linger there, finding them soft and pleasing to the touch.

Then a piercing scream sounded beside him and his hand was sent flying, as the owner of the breasts leaped to her feet. She cursed her attacker, calling him a thief, a rapist and the Devil. Wailing and shrieking erupted on the terrace and Hussein felt his face flush, as he recognised that the voice of the woman whose breasts he had touched belonged to his wife's friend Touria.

'May God forgive me Touria,' he cried, trying to make himself heard above the screams.

'Hussein?' said Touria, her voice softening as she realised that she wasn't in any danger. 'Hussein is that you?'

'Hussein? Why Hussein!'

Hussein heard the familiar voice of his wife ringing out from the other side of the terrace. 'Mama?' he shouted, 'Thank God that you are safe and well.'

'What on earth is going on?' Mama made her way across the terrace to join Touria and her husband, as he tried to explain his misdemeanour.

'I was worried when you didn't come home,' he said, 'so I was trying to feel and smell if you were sleeping on the terrace. But I came across Touria instead and I accidentally touched her... I accidently touched her...'

'God preserve and protect us!' cried Mama. 'My dear Touria, what must you think of my foolish husband.'

'There is no harm done,' said Touria. 'All that matters is that you are safe and well and Hussein found you.'

'May God grant you forgiveness as easily as Touria,' said Mama sternly and she helped her husband to his feet.

The other women on the terrace had quietened down so that they could listen in to the conversation. Mama didn't want to give them any more gossip than was necessary, so she announced that she and Hussein would leave them in peace and she led her husband away.

As soon as they were out of earshot Mama gave in to laughter. 'My poor dear Touria,' she sighed, 'that's the first time her breasts have been touched since her husband died, God rest his soul. I can only imagine what desires you will have aroused in her now.' She shook her head and laughed again, 'You're a wicked man Hussein! And I do love you so.'

Hussein loved her too. He loved her for her loyalty and her laughter. He loved her fleshy buttocks and thighs, her full breasts and her sweet smell.

Yet over the coming days he couldn't help himself, just occasionally, thinking back to the feel of Touria's small pleasing bosom.

A PLACE TO REST

The coach rounded a corner and Fatiha opened her eyes. It was close to midnight and the town was deserted. She and her brother Hamou were making their way across the country to visit relatives. They had left their village on the other side of the mountains as the sun was setting and she had slept through most of the journey.

As the coach pulled into the station Fatiha stared out of the window.

'Are we getting off?' she asked.

'We're getting off,' said Hamou, 'in the name of God.'

The station was heaving with teenage boys and old men, loading and unloading the bags and boxes that were piled high on top of each coach. Hamou and Fatiha retrieved their case and pushed through the bodies to make their way out of the station.

Outside the station there was not a soul to be seen. Fatiha looked out across a square filled with row after row of small blue taxis. On the other side was a tall hotel. It didn't look inviting, but Fatiha was tired and needed somewhere to lie down.

She looked at Hamou and he nodded, 'May God protect us.'

'Amen.' Fatiha followed Hamou as he weaved his way through the taxis.

Inside the hotel they found an old man sitting behind the reception desk. He was listening to the Quran whilst smoking a cheap cigarette.

'Peace be upon you,' said Hamou.

'And upon you,' replied the old man, without looking at him.

'How much do you charge for two single rooms?'

The old man raised his head. 'Sorry son, all our rooms are taken tonight. We don't see tourists in this town, so we don't have many hotels. There's a decent one on the corner of the main road, but it isn't cheap. You'd be better off getting a taxi to Avenue Mohamed VI.' The old man looked down again.

'May God have mercy on you,' said Hamou.

They came back out onto the square. The coach station and taxi rank had both emptied during the few minutes which they had spent inside the hotel.

'Without money you are nothing in this world,' said Hamou quietly.

'We have God,' said Fatiha, 'We have everything.'

Hamou looked at his sister. 'May God forgive me.'

'Come on,' she said, 'we need a taxi, let's head for the main road.'

They walked in silence across the square and around the corner, where a small blue taxi appeared. It pulled up alongside them and the front door swung open. Together they bent down to see the driver inside.

'Peace be upon you,' they said in chorus.

'And upon you,' replied the young driver.

'Could you take us to Avenue Mohamed VI?' asked Hamou, 'My sister and I are looking for a cheap hotel where we can stay the night.'

The taxi driver put their case into the boot of the taxi and opened the back door for Fatiha. She climbed in, stretched out on the seat and closed her eyes. Hamou sat down next to the driver.

'Avenue Mohamed VI?' he asked.

'God willing,' replied the taxi driver. 'There are a couple of hotels we can try. I'm Younis by the way.'

'Hamou and Fatiha, we're honoured to meet you.'

'The honour is mine.'

They drove away from the square, passing down a long wide avenue, which was home to the town's banks, post office and town hall. Gradually the street narrowed and the buildings became smaller and dirtier. Younis pulled up outside one with a row of lights above the door. Fatiha, who had fallen asleep, was roused by the lights shining into the taxi.

Hamou turned around to face his sister. 'Are you still tired?'

'Yes,' said Fatiha, 'The coach journey must have worn me out.'

'You wait here with Younis,' he said, 'while I see if there are any rooms.' He got out of the taxi and disappeared inside the hotel.

'I've also got a sister about your age,' said Younis, as he looked intently at the door of the hotel. 'Zaynab. She's getting married this summer, then she'll be heading north to live with her husband's family.'

'I've never been to the north,' said Fatiha. 'They say it's like Europe.'

A group of young boys ran past the taxi and Younis spat in disgust. 'They're only kids, but they're already addicted to every drug you can find in this town.' He moved round in his seat as he followed the boys. 'They never show their faces in daylight. I would never see them if I didn't spend my nights driving this taxi.'

Fatiha remembered the night before they left home. Hamou had unnerved her with stories of muggings and robberies which his friends had brought back from this town. She had pointed out to him that they were simply stories.

They were interrupted by Hamou opening the taxi door and climbing back into his seat.

'No rooms?' asked Younis.

'There are plenty of rooms,' said Hamou, 'but apparently not for Fatiha.'

Younis smiled. 'We're not used to women travellers in these parts,' he said, 'The only women you'll find in our hotels are prostitutes.'

He started up the taxi and drove a short distance further down the street, stopping in front of a sign with a badly painted camel on it. Hamou climbed out of the taxi and disappeared behind another closed door. He reappeared after only a few seconds and dropped into his seat facing Younis and Fatiha.

'The four rooms which they have allocated for women have all been taken,' he said laughing. Younis laughed too.

Fatiha didn't laugh. She needed to sleep. She rested her head against the window and studied another group of young boys who had turned into the street. Then Younis twisted round in his seat, so that he could see both Fatiha and Hamou. Fatiha turned away from the boys to face him.

'My parents live in the mountains,' he said, 'but when I've been working all night I often don't want the long drive home. So I rent a room not far from here. It's nothing special, but if you don't mind sharing a room then you are both welcome to spend the night there.'

'May God reward you for this,' said Hamou.

'May God protect you,' said Fatiha.

'You don't need to thank me,' said Younis, 'it's

my duty. After all, Fatiha looks like she needs to sleep and I feel I've been called on to find you both a place to rest.'

Younis shuffled back into his seat and started the engine. He turned off the main street and manoeuvred the taxi down a series of narrow passages. Fatiha watched as they passed by the town's mechanics and carpenters, cobblers and tailors. Then Younis slowed the taxi down and parked it between two garages.

The three of them got out of the taxi and Fatiha and Hamou followed Younis up to a tiny wooden door. He unlocked it and led them inside into darkness. When he turned on the light they saw another door at the end of the hall. Younis unlocked this door with some difficulty and beckoned to them to follow him.

Hamou and then Fatiha edged their way inside. The room was small and empty. It reminded Fatiha of the room at home where she and her sisters slept every night.

Hamou turned to Younis. 'May God reward you for all your efforts tonight. It will be an honour and a privilege for us to sleep in your home.'

'May God grant you a long life,' said Fatiha.

'I'll be back in the morning when I've finished my shift,' said Younis, 'and I'll bring breakfast. Goodnight to you both. May God wake you in good health in the morning.'

'Amen,' said Hamou.

Younis went out and closed the door behind him. Fatiha was so tired that she felt she could fall asleep on the cold bare floor. But she pulled out djellabas and jumpers from their case and arranged them to make a bed. She took out a set of prayer beads and placed them under the jumper that would be her pillow. Her grandmother had given them to her before she left, saying they would protect her on the journey.

'God has taken good care of us tonight,' said Hamou. 'You can sleep now sister. In the name of God the most merciful.'

They both lay down on their makeshift bed. Fatiha closed her eyes, finally able to rest her tired body. She instantly fell asleep.

Hamou placed his mobile phone and leather-bound Quran next to his pillow, as he did every night. He too would soon fall asleep, but first he silently recited some short verses from the end of the Quran.

As for Fatiha, she had reached the end of her journey. She passed away peacefully in her sleep, as the words of the Holy Quran laid her to rest.

SAID AND THE CAMELS

Said held his stick in the air and trilled at the top of his voice. He tugged on the camels' rope and improvised another song:

'Here come the camels!
Si Moh and Mimoun, Amlal and Miloud.
The day will soon be over, our stomachs will be full
and God willing we will sleep a good night's sleep.'

He took out his phone to check the hour. The sun would soon be setting and he wanted to set up camp for the night before it grew dark. He whistled a tune as he looked to his left and right and then decided to change course. Steering the camels to the west he increased his pace, pushing himself along with his stick. He kept a firm grip on the camels' rope as he continued with his song:

*'The camels were born in the finest of sands
and believed they were destined to carry
kings and sultans.
Instead they carry bottles of water
and blankets and pans,
and tourists whose soft buttocks bruise
with each landing on the camels' backs.'*

The four camels slowly climbed the steep bank of a dune, stretched out in a row behind Said. They descended the other side at a trot, pulling Said with them. He stopped and looked around. They were in a wide valley edged with acacia trees, which would provide food for the camels and shelter for Said during the night. He spotted a much larger acacia tree standing on its own directly ahead and pulled on Si Moh's rope to signal moving on.

The sand beneath their feet was soft and they walked with slow heavy steps. Said could feel the weight of the camels pulling on the rope behind him, Si Moh followed by Mimoun followed by Amlal and finally Miloud, the youngest of the four.

They were approaching the large acacia tree, where Said had decided to rest for the night. He felt that he was pulling the camels along against their will. Amlal was barely moving his feet, so Said pulled firmly on the rope which tied Amlal's mouth to Mimoun's saddle. He then tightened the rope from Si Moh's mouth, which he had wrapped around his hand.

Si Moh and Mimoun let out a long loud moan and Amlal and Miloud responded by vigorously shaking their heads.

Said turned round to face them. 'Behave yourselves!' he reprimanded them. 'The faster we walk, the sooner we can set up our camp. Then you can be relieved of your luggage and begin dining on sun-dried dates.'

He was about to raise his voice, but he changed his mind. Instead he moved in towards Si Moh and stroked the side of the camel's head, clicking his tongue to reassure him.

Si Moh responded to his touch and became quiet and still, which in turn calmed the other camels. Said gave Si Moh the signal to move and when he did so the other three followed his lead. But after taking only a few steps, Si Moh stamped his front feet deep into the sand and stopped moving. Whereupon Mimoun, Amlal and Miloud did exactly the same and stood defiantly behind their leader.

Said was puzzled. He had never seen the camels behave like this. Si Moh in particular was an obedient and trustworthy animal. He couldn't imagine why he seemed to be refusing to walk up to the acacia tree. He was certain that it wasn't due to tiredness or injury.

As dusk was fast approaching he decided to leave the camels where they were and concentrate on setting up his camp. He removed the saddles from each camel in turn and could feel them relax as they realised that they wouldn't be forced to follow him. He dragged the saddles over to the acacia tree, where he made up a bed and a cooking area. In the fading light he could see the distant figures of the camels. They were still where he had left them, but they were now sitting on the ground.

Said put a pan of water to heat on the gas burner and chopped some vegetables. He picked up a sack of dried dates and walked towards the camels. They moaned as he approached and then got to their feet and huddled together. Said pushed them all back to clear a space and scattered the dates on the sand lying between them.

As he walked back to the acacia tree he was relieved to see the four of them sitting in a circle enjoying the dates. He poured some of the water which he'd heated into a small bucket, added the vegetables to the pan and walked off into the dunes to perform his ablutions. He prayed both the afternoon and sunset prayers and then knelt for a moment watching the stars come out. Aside from the occasional sound from one of the camels, the night was quiet and still.

He walked back to his camp, put a pot of tea on the heat and ate his dinner. All the while he was watching the silhouettes of the camels. They had settled down, but they still hadn't moved.

Said had known Si Moh, Amlal and Mimoun for several years and he was familiar with all of their habits and routines. In the evenings they would usually wander off in search of trees and plants to eat, but this evening they didn't seem to want to explore the valley.

Said poured himself a glass of tea and quickly drank it down. He slurped down a couple more glasses and then walked over to the camels. Despite their unusual behaviour, he couldn't risk waking in the morning to find that they'd wandered too far. So he pulled some lengths of rope from his pocket and tethered their legs.

'Goodnight and sleep well,' he said to them.

He was growing tired, so he walked back to the acacia tree and checked the time on his phone. Relieved to find that the evening prayer had passed, he returned to the spot where he'd prayed earlier and prayed his final prayer of the day. Then he walked back to the acacia tree, drank a glass of lukewarm tea and washed up the dishes that he'd used.

He pulled a blanket over his legs and lay down on his bed looking up at the stars. The camels were moaning again. He closed his eyes and listened to their refrain until he fell asleep.

In the early hours of the morning Said was woken by a deafening roar. He sat up and looked across at the camels, as his eyes adjusted to the darkness. The four of them were still lying in the same place and they all appeared to be sleeping.

Said assumed that one of them must have been dreaming and he lay back down. As he did so a wind appeared from the east and swept over him. He wrapped the blanket tightly around his body and slowly moved towards sleep. His mind mixed fragments of dream with images from the last few days. He heard the wind whisper beside him and he let the sound of the whisper float over the pictures in his mind. Then the whisper grew louder, as it was joined by other whispers which gathered around him.

Said opened his eyes. Without moving his head or his body he looked around. He was lying under the branches of the acacia tree and he could see the camels sleeping in the distance. There was no one else, not even the movement of an animal. Yet he was surrounded by the sound of human voices whispering.

Said kept his body still and tried to slow his breathing. He knew that the voices were as real as the sand underneath him, as real as the stars in the sky and he was afraid. He fixed his eyes on the camels and spoke loudly into the night:

'God is the greatest, God is the greatest.
There is only one God
and Mohamed is His prophet.
God is the greatest, God is the greatest.'

The voices continued to whisper. Said lay on his back looking up into the night and gradually grew used to his fear. Then he closed his eyes and fell asleep listening to the whispers.

In the morning Said woke as the sun was rising and he was relieved to hear only silence. He sat up and saw that the camels had finally moved from their spot. The four of them had hopped on their bound legs to the edge of the valley, where they were breakfasting on the branches of another acacia tree.

He put a pan of water on the gas burner and set off towards them. They were quiet and gentle when he greeted them and they obediently followed him back to camp. They approached the acacia tree without a sound and settled down easily on the sand. It was as though the night before had never happened.

Said quickly performed his ablutions and prayed. The camels didn't need feeding and he wasn't hungry, so he gathered up his things, packed the saddles and loaded them onto the camels' backs. He wanted to get away from the valley as quickly as possible and the camels gave him no trouble. He and his four companions walked at a steady pace and they reached the edge of town just after midday.

In the evening Said went to the café where he spent much of his time when he wasn't in the desert.

He sat down next to a group of old men and ordered a pot of tea. He greeted each man in turn and asked after their wives and children. Then he told them the story of the camels and the whispering voices. When he had finished, the old men nodded and murmured. Then one of them spoke:

'Many years ago, in the days before our people knew the word of God, a desert village lay in the valley where you camped. One day the village was ambushed by a rival tribe and all the villagers and their animals were slaughtered. When the elders from a village nearby heard about the massacre, they sent their sons to bury the corpses.

But the murdered villagers had passed from this world in a state of ignorance and darkness. So they have never been able to find peace and rest in their passing. Instead they remain trapped, somewhere between this world and the next.

I've heard it said that the large acacia tree marks the grave where the villagers were buried. There are stories told of men hearing their voices and fleeing in fear, leaving them forever at the mercy of whatever they had disturbed.

Only God knows if this is true. But if it is, then your camels will have felt the presence of their restless souls. I think they were trying to warn you to keep away. But when you called on the Highest protection, those poor souls will have felt a fear much greater than yours.'

The old man took a sip of tea and looked up at Said. 'Those camels must have enormous respect for you as their master, to have put themselves in danger so that they could stay by your side.'

Said looked back at the old man. He drained his glass and stood. 'Not nearly as much as I have for them,' he said.

He placed his hand on his heart and bowed his head towards the old men, then walked out into the busy street.

FAITH

The old man roams the villages which encircle the town, tapping on the ground with a heavy wooden stick. He shouts out praise for God and asks forgiveness for us all. He knocks on every door that he passes and each one of these doors is opened by a woman, holding a loaf of bread or a bowl of stew or a glass of tea or some fruit.

The old man doesn't enter any of the homes. Whenever possible he takes the food away with him, otherwise he eats and drinks outside the front door, before handing back the bowl or the glass.

If he seems somewhat ungrateful, it is simply that he knows that he has the right to eat and to drink. He knows that God will provide.

TOUDA'S MARRIAGE

Touda grew up with her mother, father and two younger brothers in a small village at the foot of the mountains. From a young age she spent her days helping her mother in the home. She never went to school, as her father didn't believe that girls needed an education. He explained to her that after she married she would leave home to live with her husband, where she would be responsible for taking care of her new family.

Touda didn't take life too seriously and she never gave her worries a home. She would laugh and joke and sing as she carried out her work, entertaining her mother's friends who came round to drink tea and share gossip. On the rare occasions when she was left alone with time to herself, she would try to imagine what lay ahead for her in the future. What kind of man was she destined to marry? How many children would they have? Would she be blessed with a son?

When Touda was thirteen years old, a young man called Mohamed came to the house and asked her father for permission to marry his only daughter. His family lived in the neighbouring village and had known Touda's family for several generations.

Mohamed had spent the last three years living and working in the desert, grazing young camels until they were ready to sell at the camel market. Over time he had grown to love the nomadic life and he was looking for a girl who would be willing to raise a family with him in the desert.

Touda's father gave Mohamed his blessing and Touda was happy to do as her father wished. For she had fallen in love with Mohamed's face and his beautiful smile.

As the wedding approached she looked forward to becoming Mohamed's wife. It didn't trouble her that they would be living in the desert, and unlike many girls of her age she felt no fear at the thought of giving her body to Mohamed. When the two of them were left alone on the first night of their wedding, she embraced her new husband and her new life wholeheartedly. As the women rejoiced before the bloodied sheet hanging out of their window, Mohamed held her in his arms and she laughed at the stories he told about his childhood.

Life in the desert was unlike anything that Touda had known before. She had left her family home knowing little of the world which lay on the other side of her front door. It was the first time that she had gone beyond the outskirts of her village and it was the first time that she had experienced life without her mother by her side.

Touda's days were long and lonely. Mohamed was away working with the camels from early in the morning until late in the evening, leaving Touda alone in their tent. For a few months of each year they camped alongside other families, but most of the time she and Mohamed lived alone. There were no neighbours to call round for a chat, no sounds of the call to prayer or children playing to break the silence. Touda's only company during the day were the goats which they owned.

Touda had never before known loneliness. She missed her family and sometimes cried when Mohamed wasn't there to see her. She felt lonely even when they were living amongst other families. Neither she nor Mohamed had been born into the desert. It set her apart from the other women who had never experienced life in a town or village and so couldn't understand many of Touda's feelings.

But Touda never felt pity for herself and her love for Mohamed never wavered. At the end of each day she would lie in his arms and forget her sadness for a while, as she laughed at his jokes and lost herself in the stories he told of imaginary lands and tribes.

It was a love which gave Touda strength during

the first difficult months. And then she fell pregnant and realised that with a child inside her, she would never again be alone. The desert no longer seemed quite so forbidding and she found that she could forgive the hardships that she had suffered in it. She remembered and understood the words of her father. Her purpose in life was to take care of her new family.

As the birth grew near, Touda wished that she could have her mother by her side. She feared that she couldn't trust her body to safely deliver her son or daughter. So she and Mohamed moved to a camp with several other families, where Touda was approached by an old woman who offered to help her with the birth. When the time arrived, she placed her trust in the old woman and in God. Neither let her down and she gave birth to a healthy son, whom they named Ahmed.

Touda and Ahmed spent their days together. Touda sang as she worked and when Ahmed was old enough he joined in, drumming out rhythms on a metal tea tray. He enjoyed playing with other children, but he was just as happy playing on his own or helping his mother with her work.

By now Touda hadn't seen her family for a long time. Her mother and father had yet to meet their grandson. She had no sense of how far she had travelled from her village and she sometimes wondered how many days it would take her to walk home. It concerned her in case Ahmed should fall ill and need to see a doctor.

But it was Mohamed who was to suffer this fate. Touda had noticed that he was losing weight. She assumed that he was working too hard and eating too little, so she insisted that he ate a good breakfast each morning before he headed off with the camels. And when he returned again in the evening she wouldn't let him sleep until he had eaten dinner.

But Mohamed continued to lose weight. Then gradually he lost his appetite and Touda was unable to persuade him to eat. He grew weak and tired and no longer laughed or told her stories. He struggled to get out of bed and couldn't continue with his work. Touda managed to encourage him to sip a little milk each day, but when she looked at her husband she saw a sick man.

Mohamed had fallen ill while they were camping on their own, so Touda had no one who she could turn to for support. She decided that she and her family must leave the desert and return home. She needed to take Mohamed to a doctor and she had to try to protect Ahmed.

When she told Mohamed of her decision he didn't protest. She packed up the few items that she thought they would need, leaving behind their tent and most of their belongings. She tied the goats together with rope so that Ahmed could steer them, and she helped support Mohamed so that he could walk.

Touda tried to encourage her son to laugh and

sing, in the hope that it might distract him from his worries about his father. But she couldn't hide from him the fact that Mohamed was barely able to stand and that she was growing weak from bearing his weight. As she fell asleep each night Touda feared for her family.

It took them three days to reach the nearest well. They set up camp in the open air and Touda spread the word that they were looking for transport to the nearest town. A few days later a small van approached and a market trader offered them a lift back to her village.

When Touda arrived at her family home she was dismayed to find that there was no room for her new family. Her two brothers had brought wives and then children into the home and the house was full.

Mohamed was by now gravely ill and for the first time Touda felt something close to despair. Then an aunt who was visiting at the time took pity on her. She invited Touda and her family to take shelter in a small shack, which her husband had built in their garden using palm fronds. Touda gave her aunt the goats which they owned, to thank her for her kindness.

The aunt lived on the other side of town, so Touda's brothers carried Mohamed to a taxi and rode with him to the house. There they carried him through the garden and into the small shack that was to be Touda's new home.

Touda and Ahmed arrived in a second taxi, carrying their few possessions. They sat with Mohamed, who was moving in and out of consciousness. A doctor from the village came and examined him. He told Touda that Mohamed was beyond the help of a hospital and prescribed some tablets instead. But Mohamed was no longer able to swallow, so Touda would dip her finger in milk and rub it onto his lips.

Touda knew that her husband was dying. She tried to shield Ahmed from what was happening, but she sensed that he too understood. She didn't sleep for several days, fearful of missing her last moments with her husband.

When Mohamed died in the early hours of the morning, she was lying awake beside him and heard him slip away. She kissed him on the lips and forehead and said a prayer over him. Ahmed was sleeping and she didn't wake him. She stood up to go and tell her aunt that Mohamed was gone and her legs gave way beneath her.

It was then that Touda cried.

SI ABDALLAH'S SUSPICION

Si Abdallah was tired. He was too old to be spending his days lifting heavy bags up onto the backs of camels and promenading tourists under a hot desert sun. At the end of each day his body ached and he wasn't sure how much longer it would cope with the demands of his work.

It wasn't that he disliked the tourists that he worked with. On the contrary, he found that most were kind and charming and it was a pleasure to spend time with them. It was simply that he had hoped for a rest in his later years.

The other desert guides were young and fit and would go on to better things. But Si Abdallah had long ago given up such hopes. For God had decreed that he and his wife would only bring daughters into the world. So with no son to relieve him of the responsibility of providing for his family, Si

Abdallah had been forced to continue working into his old age.

On the day in question Monsieur and Madame were a middle-aged French couple visiting the desert for the first time. They seemed cheerful and relaxed and Si Abdallah imagined that it would be an easy day's work. He greeted them both and introduced them to the two camels who would be taking them on their tour of the dunes. Then he knelt down on one knee beside the smaller of the camels and held out his arms, inviting Madame to climb up onto the camel's back.

Madame hoisted herself up and the camel groaned and snorted, swishing its belly from side to side as though trying to shake her off.

'Are you comfortable Madame?' Si Abdallah tugged at one of the blankets and adjusted the saddle. 'Madame, are you comfortable?'

Madame nodded and smiled, as she fiddled with the scarf which he had wound around her head.

Si Abdallah bent down and untied the camel's right legs, then walked round and untied the left. He gave the command for the camel to push itself up into a standing position. The camel flexed its back legs and Madame went hurtling forward head first, sliding down the camel's neck and head shrieking in French, before landing heavily and awkwardly on the ground.

'God help us, Madame!' Si Abdallah ran over to

Madame, who stared back at him with no expression on her face. 'Madame? Madame, are you hurt? Oh dear God.'

Si Abdallah rushed to get a bottle of water from the camel's saddle. As he did so he became aware of a strange squealing sound coming from behind him.

When he turned around he was shocked to see Monsieur lying on his back in the sand, howling with laughter.

'Ah Monsieur Abdul,' he spluttered, 'My poor wife, I fear she is not comfortable at all!' At which Monsieur gave in to another convulsion of laughter.

Si Abdallah stared at Monsieur. It was then that he realised that he had neglected to tell Madame to take hold of the handles on the saddle, before he gave the command for the camel to stand.

He turned back to look at poor Madame and he wondered. Was he simply becoming forgetful in his old age? Or had a tired old man finally succumbed to a desire to rebel against that which God had decreed?

ABDERRAHMANE

Abderrahmane crawled through the town on his hands and knees, his crippled feet lifted off the ground. He had been crawling like this for as long as anyone could remember, slowly making his way along the dusty pavements until he found a suitable place to sit for a while. He was happiest when sitting and watching, occasionally chatting to the people who passed by.

He had never begged in the street. He had never asked anyone for anything. He had found that there were many kind people in this town and that they were never far from his reach. The shopkeepers and café owners kept him supplied with sweet tea and hot food and let him sleep in their premises during the winter. Beyond that there was very little that he needed.

It was early morning and Abderrahmane was

making his way up a narrow flight of steps. As he neared the top he could see Selma, the old woman who could always be found sitting in the same spot in front of her son's house. He pulled himself up onto the top step and manoeuvred himself into a comfortable sitting position. Selma waved to him and he waved back.

From this vantage he had a good view of the busy main street and could enjoy watching the people below as they set about their business for the day. He felt reassured by the rhythms of the children making their way to school and the familiar faces of men and women who passed him every morning on their way to work.

Time moved slowly and the sun grew steadily stronger and warmer. When its rays reached the back of Abderrahmane's head, it was time for him to move on and find some shade. Selma had fallen asleep, as was her habit at this time of day, so he moved quietly past her and decided to head for the bus station.

He made his way down a steep pathway which ran between two small hotels and turned into the road which would take him to the station. The pavement was uneven and full of holes. It was a difficult surface for Abderrahmane to negotiate, so he crawled down the kerb and into the roadside to continue on his way.

The pavement on the other side of the road was wide and filled with tables and chairs from the cafés which lined its route. Fatima-Zohra was sitting outside one of the cafés. She'd caught the first bus into town so she could buy some new clothes from the outdoor market. It was the largest market in the area and families travelled long distances to stock up on clothing and household goods, weighing down taxis and buses with their bags. Fatima-Zohra had bought dresses for her mother and daughters, and was drinking a coffee to pass the time until she could catch her bus home.

It wasn't yet time for lunch, so the tables around her were empty and the pavements had yet to be filled with school children and workers making their way home. Fatima-Zohra was enjoying the quiet, watching the cars and taxis passing by, when she spotted Abderrahmane crawling along the side of the road. She moved quickly from her seat, assuming that he was unwell or had fallen out of a passing vehicle. She kept losing sight of him, as cars and taxis continued to pass by in front of her. And then the traffic eased and she saw that Abderrahmane was crawling along the side of the road because he was crippled.

She took her purse from her bag and put a few coins on the table beside her half-empty glass. Abderrahmane was almost in front of her now. She stood and walked to the edge of the pavement, waited for a gap in the traffic and crossed to the other side of the road. As Abderrahmane approached her, she walked towards him.

'Peace be upon you,' she said warmly.

'And upon you peace,' he replied, continuing his steady crawl.

'Where are you heading?' she asked.

'To the bus station, God willing,' he replied, still crawling.

Fatima-Zohra took her purse out of her bag and pulled out a handful of coins. 'In the name of God,' she said, 'let me pay for a taxi to take you there.'

Abderrahmane stopped moving and looked directly at her. 'Thank you Madam,' he said, 'but I prefer to make my own way. I'm in no hurry. I'm going to the station to sit and rest in the shade of a tree. And the tree isn't going anywhere.'

Fatima-Zohra held out her hand with the coins in it. 'Then please, just take the money. Buy yourself something to eat.'

Abderrahmane smiled and shook his head. 'Thank you again Madam. But I have no need for money.'

He bowed his head and resumed his crawling along the edge of the road. Fatima-Zohra let her eyes follow him, as she slowly realised what Abderrahmane had just said.

THE PILGRIM AND THE ALCOHOLIC

Si Hamed and Si Brahim lived in a small shanty town which lay on a hillside overlooking the sea.

Si Hamed worked as a scribe in the main town and was a popular and respected figure in the community. He was a devoutly religious man. He prayed every day in the local mosque and was often to be found reciting the Quran over friends and neighbours, for his door was always open to anyone in need.

Though he wasn't well acquainted with his neighbour Si Brahim, like everyone else in the shanty town he had heard stories about the poor man's drinking. Si Brahim, like most of his neighbours, worked at the local factory. But it seemed to those around him that he wasted all of the money that he earned on whisky. For each day he would return home from work and spend his evening drinking whisky in front of the television until he passed out.

Over the years his life had been reduced to little more than drinking. He no longer sat in the cafés chatting with friends and had long ago lost touch with his family in the mountains.

But what Si Hamed and the rest of the shanty town didn't know was that Si Brahim had a secret. Next door to him there lived a young woman who had been widowed a few years after getting married. She had been left with two small children to care for, but she had no money and no family to help her out. Si Brahim barely knew her and he had no interest in taking her as his wife, but his heart had gone out to her two children. So one day he had knocked on the young widow's door and given her his word that, for as long as they needed and he was able, he would take care of her and her children. In return he asked only that she say nothing of the arrangement to anyone else.

She had obliged and had told no one about Si Brahim's generosity. And so at the end of each month, when the factory owner handed Si Brahim his modest wage, he would first deliver half of the sum to the young widow who lived next door, before squandering the rest on his beloved whisky.

It so happened that Si Hamed had also been quietly living on much less than he was earning. For several years he had been putting money aside, in the hope that he would one day be able to make the sacred pilgrimage. He had finally amassed the sum of money which he needed and his forthcoming trip was the talk of the shanty town. When the day of his departure arrived all of his neighbours gathered to wave him off, including Si Brahim who was standing on the edge of the crowd.

When Si Hamed reached The Holy City of Mecca he had never before seen so many people. His eyes filled with tears and his heart filled with love and devotion. He felt changed from the very first moment and knew that he was about to experience the most important days of his life.

Si Hamed immersed himself deeply in the prayer and ritual of his pilgrimage. Then on the third day he saw a face in the crowd ahead of him which looked familiar. The man in question kept looking to his left and right, showing only his profile, and it took a few moments for Si Hamed to recognise him. But when he did so he realised that he was looking at his neighbour Si Brahim.

Of course Si Hamed knew that it couldn't possibly be poor Si Brahim the alcoholic. But it did look remarkably like him. If he had believed in such things he would have assumed that the man was Si Brahim's identical twin, walking the earth living out his alternative life. Then the Si Brahim lookalike turned his head and Si Hamed shivered. For this was surely and without a doubt his neighbour Si Brahim the alcoholic.

Si Hamed pushed past the pilgrims in front of

him, feeling shame at his own rudeness. The pilgrims behind were pushing into him and propelling him forward. He feared losing his footing or being trampled by the crowd. He was determined to reach Si Brahim, but the crowd overwhelmed him and Si Brahim was lost amongst the other pilgrims.

Later that night Si Hamed dreamed about Si Brahim walking through the streets of the shanty town. But the next day he couldn't see his neighbour anywhere in the crowd. So he put the matter aside and surrendered to the sublime act of pilgrimage.

However as soon as Si Hamed arrived back home he went round to see Si Brahim. He told his neighbour the story of how he saw his likeness in The Holy City of Mecca. 'I know that you are an alcoholic,' he said, 'but I believe that you are a good man and that you accompanied me on my pilgrimage.'

Si Brahim looked at his neighbour and was moved by Si Hamed's faith in him. 'Tomorrow morning,' he said, 'when you walk past my house on your way to pray in the mosque, call for me and I will join you.'

'God willing,' said Si Hamed, 'That will give me great pleasure.'

That evening Si Brahim left his bottle of whisky unopened. He watched television for a while and then went to the bathroom, where he repeatedly doused his head and body in water. He retired to bed early and slept peacefully until Si Hamed knocked on his door the following morning.

When Si Brahim arrived at the mosque he could feel the other worshippers watching him, and as he carried out his ablutions he could hear them whispering. But Si Hamed chatted to him as though they regularly attended the mosque together and slowly the atmosphere changed. Men came up and shook his hand and he felt welcomed. He followed Si Hamed into the prayer hall and there he prayed the first prayer of his adult life.

Afterwards he went on to his work at the factory and he joined his colleagues when they broke off to pray the midday and afternoon prayers. At home in the evening he again refrained from drinking whisky. Instead he cooked himself a meal and at the appointed times he prayed the sunset and evening prayers. Once again he retired early and slept peacefully until Si Hamed knocked on his door in the morning.

Si Brahim was surprised to find that sobriety came easily and naturally. He enjoyed his new routine and felt all the better for it. His body was healthier and his mind less troubled.

One morning he woke early and went for a walk on the beach. He had an hour or so before he needed to head home to get ready for the mosque, so he decided to have a swim in the sea. He hadn't been in the sea since he was a child and he had fond memories of swimming with his father.

But Si Brahim was blind to the dangers of the tide and the current. The cold of the early morning water gave him a cramp in one of his legs and his poor body, which had been weakened by years of drinking whisky, couldn't fight it. When a strong current pulled him under he was no match for the power of the sea. A few hours later a fisherman came across his body lying at the edge of the water.

When Si Hamed heard what had happened to Si Brahim he was heartbroken. Then he got down on his knees, bowed his head and thanked God for bringing his friend into the fold before releasing him from this world.

A GUEST IN THEIR HOME

Rqiyya watched a lizard run across the wall and disappear behind a pile of clothes. She had woken more than an hour ago, but had yet to make the effort to get out of bed. The August heat was intense and she felt she needed a little more sleep. So she drank the water from the glass beside her bed and closed her eyes.

She woke some time later and looked around the room. The light had changed while she had been sleeping, lengthening the shadows that stretched behind the glass and the bottle of water beside it.

Her body felt uncomfortable, so she rolled onto her side. She touched her forehead and then her arms and thighs. There was a fire burning beneath her skin, but there was no sweat on its surface.

She filled another glass with water and lay on her back. Her hands shook as she slowly dribbled the water onto her forehead, letting it run down into her hair and onto the pillow.

She had no desire to move, but she needed to get to the bathroom. So she pushed herself up off the bed and walked unsteadily across the room. When she reached the bathroom she crouched over the hole in the ground and vomited.

She lay on the bathroom floor until she felt strong enough to stand. Then she walked back to her room, lay down and slept some more. When she woke again she rested for a while with her eyes closed, feeling in no hurry to let in the light of day. But she could feel a force urging her to return to the room and she was compelled to surrender to it.

When she opened her eyes she found Mimi the cat sitting beside her, staring up at the ceiling behind her head. She reached out and stroked the back of Mimi's neck. This was usually Mimi's cue to snuggle up to her, but the cat didn't respond. She ignored Rqiyya's touch and continued to stare up at the ceiling.

'What is there Mimi?' She followed the line of Mimi's stare, tilting her head back on the pillow to look up at the ceiling.

Rqiyya heard herself scream. She was looking up at an old man and a group of old women, who were floating above her head with their backs pushed up against the ceiling. They were neither naked nor clothed. They were talking quietly amongst themselves and didn't appear to have heard her screams. They didn't seem to know that Rqiyya was lying on the bed beneath them.

Rqiyya felt her body grow cold. Her instinct was to flee the house, but she couldn't move. Her neck was locked in place and her eyelids were fixed open. She could only stare up at the terrifying scene.

Then to her horror the old man turned his head and looked down at her, and she had no choice but to look back at him. Staring into his eyes she felt a growing pressure against her chest. She struggled to inflate and empty her lungs. She could feel the weight of the bodies on the ceiling pressing down on her and she feared that she would choke. Sucking in a deep breath, she held onto it for as long as she could before letting it go.

Rqiyya felt that she had been absent for a while. She was looking up at the ceiling, but the old man had turned his attention away from her and was whispering to some of the old women.

She slowly lifted her head and saw that Mimi had fallen asleep at the bottom of her bed. Looking around the room it seemed to her that every familiar object was in its place. When she breathed in she could faintly smell the incense which perfumed her clothes.

Rqiyya looked back at the old man and the old

women and realised that their presence no longer frightened her. She felt safe lying beneath them.

She turned back to look at Mimi and watched the cat's body moving gently up and down with each breath. It was then that she remembered something which her grandfather had once told her. He had said that the blessings in life often frighten us when they first appear, for we can be slow to recognise their true nature.

She understood now that the old man and the old women had been living in the house for many more years than her. She was their guest, a visitor passing through. When they saw that she had fallen ill, they had appeared before her so that they might heal her.

Rqiyya rested her head on the pillow and closed her eyes once more. She knew that when she was well enough to return, the old man would safely show her the way back.

ACKNOWLEDGEMENTS

I would like to thank Andrew Franks, Ray Batchelor, my partner Al and my Moroccan family, without whom these stories would not have been realised.

SOUL BAY PRESS
LONDON EASTBOURNE SYDNEY
MMXV